# Jessica's Two Dads



By Melvin J. Coates

Illustrated By: Scribbleline

Once upon a time, in a cozy little town nestled in the mountains, there lived **a young girl named Jessica. She had** big brown eyes, a smile that could light up a room, and two dads who loved her more than anything in the world.

Many of the other kids at school had just one mom or dad, and sometimes Jessica would wonder why she was different. She knew that her dads loved each other very much, and they had always told her that they wanted her to be a part of their family. But Jessica still couldn't help but wonder why she had two dads instead of a mom and a dad like everyone else.

One day, Jessica mustered up the courage to ask her dads about it. "Why do I have two dads instead of a mom and a dad like everyone else?" she asked.

Her dads smiled at each other and held hands. "Well, Jessica," said her dad, "it's because your other dad and I are both men. We love each other very much, just like any other mom and dad would. And we wanted to have a child together to make our family complete."

Jessica thought about this for a moment. "But how did I come to be if you're both men?" she asked. Her dads explained that there are many different ways for people to have children, and that they had chosen to use a special process called surrogacy.

This meant that a kind woman had carried a baby for them, and when the baby was born, they became Jessica's legal parents.

Jessica's eyes lit up with understanding. "So I have two dads because you both wanted to be my parents, and you used surrogacy to make it happen?"

Her dads nodded and hugged her tightly. "Exactly, sweetheart. And we wouldn't have it any other way. You're the best thing that's ever happened to us."

Jessica smiled, feeling loved and accepted. She realized that having two dads didn't make her any different from other kids – it just meant that she had twice as much love and support in her life.

But not everyone in the town felt
the same way. Some people didn't
understand why Jessica had two dads,
and they would make fun of her or
say mean things. Jessica didn't
understand why they were being
so unkind, and it made her feel
sad and confused.

Rainbow Center

One day, Jessica's dads took her to a special place called the Rainbow Center. It was a place where people who were part of the LGBTQ+ community could come to find support and acceptance. There, Jessica met other kids who had two moms or two dads, and she realized that she wasn't alone.

She also met a kind lady named Sarah, who was a counselor at the Rainbow Center. Sarah helped Jessica understand that everyone is different, and that's what makes the world such a wonderful place. She told Jessica that just because some people might not understand or accept her family, it didn't mean they were wrong or that there was anything wrong with her.

Jessica felt a weight lift off her shoulders as she listened to Sarah's words. She realized that having two dads wasn't something to be ashamed of – it was something to be proud of. She went home feeling confident and loved, knowing that her dads were the best parents anyone could ask for.

As Jessica grew older, she learned more and more about the LGBTQ+ community and the struggles that people like her dads had faced in the past. She learned about the Stonewall Riots, where brave LGBTQ+ people stood up for their rights and started a movement that would change the world. She learned about the rainbow flag, which symbolized the diversity and acceptance of the LGBTQ members

To Be Continued

# EXPLORE THE WORLD OF **MELVIN COATES**

PUBLISHER : RENEGADE

## Discover Engaging Stories

books.melvincoates.com

**SCAN TO LEAVE A REVIEW**
**YOUR FEEDBACK MATTERS**